REAPER'S RIDE
BROTHERHOOD PROTECTORS WORLD

DELILAH DEVLIN

Copyright © 2018, Delilah Devlin

This book is a work of fiction. Names, characters, places and incidents are products of the author's imagination or used fictitiously. Any resemblance to actual events, locales or persons living or dead is entirely coincidental.

© 2018 Twisted Page Press, LLC ALL RIGHTS RESERVED

No part of this book may be used, stored, reproduced or transmitted without written permission from the publisher except for brief quotations for review purposes as permitted by law.

This book is licensed for your personal enjoyment only. This book may not be re-sold or given away to other people. If you would like to share this book with another person, please purchase an additional copy for each recipient. If you're reading this book and did not purchase it, or it was not purchased for your use only, please purchase your own copy.

Note: This book was previously released through Amazon Kindle World.

BROTHERHOOD PROTECTORS

ORIGINAL SERIES BY ELLE JAMES

Brotherhood Protectors Series
Montana SEAL (#1)
Bride Protector SEAL (#2)
Montana D-Force (#3)
Cowboy D-Force (#4)
Montana Ranger (#5)
Montana Dog Soldier (#6)
Montana SEAL Daddy (#7)
Montana Ranger's Wedding Vow (#8)
Montana SEAL Undercover Daddy (#9)
Cape Cod SEAL Rescue (#10)
Montana SEAL Friendly Fire (#11)
Montana SEAL's Bride (#12)
Montana Rescue
Hot SEAL, Salty Dog

ABOUT THE BOOK

Reaper's Ride
A Montana Bounty Hunters Story
Delilah Devlin

Badass Montana bounty hunter, Reaper Stenberg, is a take-*all*-prisoners kind of guy and goes balls-to-the-wall in every capture. Until he's injured. The last thing he wants to admit is any vulnerability. And he doesn't want to hear about it from his wife and partner, Carly. So, with a bum shoulder, he jumps headlong into the next job, working with teammates, Dagger and Lacey, to take down a dangerous arsonist. Soon, he wonders if he's taken on more than he can chew, but it might be too late to admit he needs a little help...

CHAPTER 1

REAPER SHIVERED and pulled the edge of the blanket up to his ears, grasping onto sleep, but a frigid breeze teased his nose, and his ass was getting cold. He pried open scratchy eyes, noting the gray light and figured it must be near dawn. Then he lifted his head and stared through the windshield at a house, hidden in the trees farther down the lane. Where the hell was he?

Oh, right. He was staking out Bert O'Sullivan's house, hoping the bail-jumping armed robber would head home for a change of clothes or to pick up one of the weapons he kept wrapped in an old tablecloth under his bed. Reaper knew exactly where they were, because he'd already searched the house, looking for clues of Big Bert's whereabouts. Just as an added precaution, he'd removed the bolts from the rifles, should Bert sneak back inside his place before he and Carly nailed his ass.

Speaking of the woman…

He glanced to his right. Her seat was empty, which partially explained the frigid air inside his Ford Expedition. Reaper hit the button at the side of his seat and listened to the whir as the back of his seat rose. He glanced around, surprised to discover snow had fallen while he'd caught some shut-eye. A trail of footprints led into the bushes beside the road, and he smiled.

Two nights ago when they'd first arrived, he and Carly discussed the necessities of a long stakeout. He'd packed an empty liter soda bottle for relieving himself, should the need arise, and had offered her one of her own.

But she'd rolled her eyes and dug inside her knapsack for her toilet paper. "I'd rather use the bushes."

"You know they sell devices that make it easier for you to hit the target…"

"No, thanks," she'd said and lifted her chin. Subject closed.

Chuckling, he bet that right about now, she wished she could have used the coke bottle.

The clock on the dash read 6:00 AM. Dawn was breaking. Reaching for the key in the ignition, he was about to start the vehicle and warm up the seats, when he saw a compact, lights off, roll to a stop in front of Big Bert's house.

A large figure climbed out of the Prius, bouncing the small car as the male exited and slammed the door. The man looked up and down the street, his gaze snagging on Reaper's Expedition.

Reaper ducked down to watch, his heart thudding, while Big Bert looked away then made a beeline for his front door. Once the fugitive was inside the house, Reaper lowered his window. "Psst! Carly!" he whispered harshly. "Get back to the truck."

"Just a minute," she muttered.

"Don't have a minute. He's here!"

"You better not be kidding," she said, her voice rising.

"Hurry it up!"

"Son-of-a-bitch." The frost-coated bushes crackled. Carly jogged around the back of the truck, pulling up her zipper.

Reaper let himself out, eased the door closed, then hunkered down to hide behind his SUV as he made his way to the back gate.

Carly already had the door open and rifled through his "go-bag". She donned a Kevlar vest, slid her badge onto her web belt, which held pepper spray and a lock pick kit in the loops. Then she slid a Glock into the holster strapped to her thigh.

He reached past her for his shotgun, already loaded with bean-bag rounds.

Carly shoved a vest at his chest.

Reaper didn't want to take the time to put it on. He'd already disabled Big Bert's weapons, but rather than waste precious seconds with another argument, he donned the vest and shut the door on the vehicle. Then leaning toward Carly, he gave her a frown that would have had most men backing up a step. Not his woman, though.

She shot him an equally fierce scowl. "I am not staying behind you. I'll take the back door."

He blew out a breath and gave a reluctant nod. If she was any other hunter he employed, he'd expect her to take the other entrance, but he didn't like letting her out of his sight. "You've got a weapon. Don't forget how to use it."

Shaking her head, she snorted. "I'm a better shot than you. Just don't get in my way."

"Back door's already unlocked," he reminded her. He'd left it unlatched when he'd conducted his search. "Keep quiet as you come through. I'll make enough noise to get his attention."

She slipped her fingers into her pocket, pulled out her earpiece, and tucked it into her left ear. "Got it. Let's get this bastard." She waggled her eyebrows. "Sky and Jamie are gonna be pissed they lost the coin toss."

Sky and Jamie sat on Bert's girlfriend's place. Calling them now wouldn't make any sense. The location was ten minutes away, and Reaper was pretty sure they didn't have ten minutes to cool their heels waiting for the other couple.

Together, Reaper and Carly ran from tree to tree, moving toward the small clapboard house. Painted white maybe a decade ago, the grungy, peeling paint looked as neglected as the yard, decorated with trash and rusting parts of cars, and coated with ice and fresh snowfall.

Reaper knew well the interior looked worse. A pig like Bert, who'd pistol-whipped a fast-food clerk because she hadn't emptied her cash drawer fast enough, betrayed his ugliness in every aspect of his life.

Near the house now, he indicated to Carly to head toward the back entrance. Reaper crouched low and moved to the front door. He paused once to dart his body upward and quickly glance inside a window.

Big Bert moved down the corridor leading toward the bedroom. The back door was at the end of the hallway. Reaper's stomach tightened. "He's heading to his stash of weapons. I'll make some noise to draw him out. Wait until you hear me."

"Got it," she whispered.

Reaper climbed the two steps of the small concrete porch and raised his boot. With a powerful kick, he shattered the doorframe then knocked away the splintered door, sagging on its hinges. "Bert O'Sullivan," he shouted as he jogged through the living room, "Fugitive Recovery Agent! Come out with your hands up!"

The back door cracked open, but Reaper waved Carly back. From inside the bedroom, he heard cursing. Then he heard crackling and something sliding. "Goddammit, he's goin' out the window!"

"On it," Carly said, ducking out the back door.

"Fuck!" He ran into the bedroom, leapt into the middle of the mattress and to the floor beyond, then bent to climb out of the small window, wondering how Bert had squeezed his big frame through.

Once on the ground, he followed footsteps in the snow, which led into the backyard. Entering the fenced yard, he watched Bert duck into a shed, with Carly maybe ten feet behind him. "Wait!" he said. "He might have another weapon—"

But that wasn't what Bert had gone after. The roar of an engine sounded, and a second later, a four-wheeler burst forward from the shadows.

Carly jumped to the side to avoid being run over.

Pissed now, Reaper stood in Bert's path, blocking the only exit—the narrow strip of lawn between the house and the neighbor's chain-link fence.

A sneer curved Bert's lips, and he twisted the throttle, giving his four-wheeler more gas, and sped faster toward Reaper, clearly intending to run him down.

At the last second, Reaper stepped to the side and shot out left his arm, clotheslining Bert across the chest, and knocking him off his ATV. Pain sucked the wind out of Reaper, and he bent at the waist cupping his shoulder.

Bert lay on the ground with the breath knocked out of him, wheezing.

Reaper turned his head to watch the ATV, momentum still propelling it forward, bounce against the side of the house, into the fence, and back against the siding, before coming to rest.

Carly ran to Bert and pointed her weapon toward his gut.

Still, gasping, Bert's gaze followed her action. With a roll of his eyes, he raised his hands.

"Need you to turn over on your belly, big boy," Carly snarled.

Moaning, Bert complied. "Can't breathe," he gasped.

"Don't have to, asshole. I'll sit you upright once the cuffs are on your wrists." She straddled the backs of his upper thighs and clasped a manacle on one thick wrist, and then reached and tugged on the other arm, ignoring Bert's groans, until she clicked the second in place. With jerking shoves, she moved him to his knees, and then to his feet. Snow and mud smeared Bert's face as he looked down at Carly, his gaze narrowing.

Stabs of pain matched his heart rate. Reaper forced himself to straighten. Through clenched teeth, he ground out, "Don't even think about it. She's a better shot than me, and you've already pissed her off."

Bert's head turned, and his gaze assessed Reaper's tall frame.

Reaper shook his head. "Ex-marine, buddy. It's not worth me kicking your ass."

In the end, Big Bert's shoulders sank, and his head dipped, his chin nearly touching his chest. As Carly led their fugitive to the Expedition, Reaper reached beneath his vest for his cellphone. He tapped the speed dial.

"Sky, here."

"We got him."

"Nice! Everyone, okay?"

Reaper didn't mention the fact he was pretty sure he'd dislocated his shoulder. "Since we made the grab, you two get to return him to jail in Bozeman."

Sky groaned. "Sounds fair. Meet you at the office."

The transport was fair all right. Even splitting it four ways, the bounty was generous. A judge had set Big Bert's bounty at $300,000. How the asshole had managed to raise his percentage of the cash was a mystery that would have to wait to be solved. Reaper sucked in a breath through clenched teeth. His shoulder was screaming.

CARLY STOOD in the corner of the treatment room at the county hospital, waiting for the doctor to finish writing scripts for anti-inflammatories and pain meds.

She scanned Reaper's body, noting the deep colors blossoming on his shoulders and flinched. The nurses who'd helped him out of his jacket and shirt when he'd arrived had certainly clucked over the bruises. They'd likely been drooling, too.

She couldn't blame them. She knew what they saw—a very tall, well-made brute of a man, long blond hair caught back in a ponytail, glacier blue eyes, rugged features with a square jaw, and bad-boy tattoos. His appearance had stopped her heart when she'd first met him. His strength of character and his courage had captured it.

She'd known the second Reaper hadn't charged Bert after knocking him free of his vehicle that he'd been hurt. Not badly. His shoulder had dislocated from its socket.

Listening to the gristly sounds as the doctor rotated his arm to snap it back in place, Carly grimaced. Reaper barely winced. Always the tough guy. Now, he stared, narrowing his gaze. She read his silent message. *Don't ride me about this.*

Her body tensed. *Like hell.* He wasn't invincible. He wouldn't expect *her* to take those kinds of risks. She didn't like that he seemed hell-bent on rushing toward danger, while he expected her to hang back and stay safe. He knew what she was capable of. She'd proven her mettle.

At last, the doctor left. Carly gathered Reaper's vest and coat.

Reaper stood, his machismo refusing to let him show any effort.

Prick.

"See? I'm right as rain."

She just shook her head and turned on her heel. As she walked down the corridor toward the exit, she didn't care if he had to move faster than was comfortable. Served him right. Once in the car, she smirked. He rarely let her drive. Now, he had no choice.

"We should hit the office."

She indicated to turn the car the opposite direction. "First, we have to hit the pharmacy to get your prescriptions."

"Drop them on the way."

She released a deep breath and some of her resentment. Yes, he'd been hurt, but the dumbass really did think he was Superman. Had to be humbling to discover he wasn't.

After cruising through the pharmacy's drive-thru window, they returned to the office.

Brian, the office manager, sat in his wheelchair in front of a monitor with one of the new hires, Lacey Jones, perched on the edge of the desk. They were reviewing "the list"—the database the main office in Kalispell maintained with the names and pertinent information for all the bounties available in their region.

Carly pressed her lips together and didn't dare glance at Reaper or she'd burst out laughing.

Lacey had been an "inspired" choice to partner with Dagger Renfrew. Petite and as pretty as the cheerleader she'd once been, today, she looked like a pretty, frosty-pink cupcake. Her pink mohair sweater had sparkly crystals across the shoulders. Her leggings were cream-colored, and her knee-hi boots a pale taupe. Pale blonde hair was held back by crystal slides, and her makeup looked perfect.

Carly sighed. She hadn't worn makeup in forever, and her clothes smelled musty after spending two days on stakeout inside Reaper's car, surrounded by empty cans of Pringles and soda. Ah well. She couldn't begrudge Lacey her perfection—the girl possessed crazy acting skills and a deft touch with relatives and friends of scumbags. Carly wished she was as talented.

Brian looked over his shoulder. "'Sup? Thought you two would be crashing. Sky and Jamie just dropped Bert in lockup in Bozeman. You're off the clock."

"We don't punch any damn clock," Reaper growled.

Brian shrugged. "Yeah, still, what the hell are you doing here?"

Carly wanted to know, too.

At that moment, the door to the restroom opened, and Dagger strode out. His eyebrows rose. "Thought you'd be out of commission for a while." He eyed Reaper's sling.

"Injured my left arm not my left nut."

Dagger grinned and walked toward him. He slapped Reaper's right shoulder. "So, you gonna join us? We're going after Ralph Tyson."

Carly whistled. Tyson already had three strikes before he was arrested for arson. She glanced at Lacey, who'd hopped off the desk and grinned ear to ear.

"Ralph's best friend gave him up." She bounced with excitement. "Said he's at the Elkhorn Bar in Eagle Rock."

"Did you promise him a facial?" Reaper drawled, a half-smile curving his mouth.

Lacey's laughter tinkled like a bell. "You guys aren't letting that one go, huh? Nope. I told his friend that Ralph bragged about setting fire to the community center. His friend, Andy, didn't think that was right."

Crossing his arms, Dagger snorted. "Swear his chest puffed up so much he had to have busted a seam when she told him how much she admired his *strength of character* for feeling that way. The man couldn't blurt his friend's whereabouts fast enough."

Lacey fluttered her eyelids. "Most people want to do the right thing. Some just need a little encouragement."

"Babe, he wasn't interested in doing the right thing. He wanted to impress you."

She planted a hand on her slim hip. "That's not such a bad thing. It worked out, didn't it? And, he insisted on giving me his number in case I ever needed his help again."

Dagger rolled his eyes. "She'll end up with a rolodex full of informants eager for her call."

Grinning, Carly reached across to fist-bump Lacey's delicate knuckles.

"What do you say?" Lacey glanced between Carly and Reaper. "Carl's a tough one. We could use the help."

Carly glanced at Reaper. She thought she'd figured out why he was so keen to get right back in the action. He didn't want to give her a chance to sit him down for "the talk." Okay, she'd go along. He was the one who'd be hurting. "But we take the Expedition. Reaper and I need a little shut-eye. We'll sleep while you drive."

Not waiting for Dagger's approval, Lacey nodded. "The Challenger would never hold all of us and Tyson, so yeah. Dagger hasn't had the time yet to trade in his muscle car for something more practical."

"Nag, nag, nag," Dagger said, a smile stretching his mouth.

Again, Lacey glanced at Carly then Reaper, brows wrinkled. "If we're sharing the close confines of the Expedition, you two need to hit the shower. Brian and I will get together the paperwork."

"Huh," Carly said, looking at Reaper. "I think she just said we stink."

Reaper waggled his eyebrows, wicked intent in his arctic-blue gaze.

Carly shook her head and walked away. *As if.* The stubborn man's face was pale, and his mouth was pinched. She'd give him his moment of bravado. She reached up and scratched her scalp.

"I stocked multiple products in the shower, Carly," Lacey called from behind.

"Thanks. You're an angel." Her steps quickened. Lacey took good care of the women in the office. So, she was as light as confectionary sugar. Everyone needed a little sugar sometime.

CHAPTER 2

REAPER WAS AN IDIOT. At this moment, he was ready to fess up how much he hurt. The ride to Eagle Rock had passed in a dull blur due to the pain meds he gobbled. He'd awoken with his head resting on Carly's shoulder. She'd given him a pointed stare, but otherwise she didn't ride him about his dumbass move to take this job. And he felt remorse for her, because she had to be tired, too.

His reason wasn't that they needed the money. Over the last month or so, the bounty hunting business had been good to them. They both enjoyed the challenges the work presented. Still, every time they began a new search, he started it with a burning hole in his gut, because he knew better than anyone how wrong things could go. He'd seen his old partner Jamie on her knees with a terrorist holding a gun to her head. He couldn't imagine how he'd feel seeing Carly in a similar situation.

Now seated in the Elkhorn Bar, he leaned an elbow on the table where he sat across from Carly and Dagger. They all watched Lacey from the corners of their eyes as she worked the bartender for information. Tyson was nowhere to be seen.

Carly shook her head, turning to watch Lacey, her expression admiring. "She's something," she said softly.

Reaper shot a glance at the blonde in all her "pinkness" as she smiled and tilted her head at the bartender. A whiskey sour sat on the bar in front of her. As he watched, the moment the bartender turned his back, Lacey swapped glasses with the guy sitting next to her. Obviously, she'd ordered the same drink so she could pull the swap for an empty glass. He doubted she'd taken a single sip, and yet, her laughter grew louder, and she leaned farther over the bar, blue eyes sparkling.

As for the guy next to her, he knew exactly

what she was doing, because he winked and grinned every time she passed him a free drink.

Reaper glanced around the bar to see if anyone else noticed the girl's antics, but no one seemed to watch that closely. Laughter and conversation were white noise inside this seedy bar. His attention went back to Lacey.

After watching her pretend to become inebriated and flirt with the bartender, he had to admit she had skills.

Lacey pushed up from her stool, fluttered her fingers in farewell to the two men she'd held in thrall, and sauntered toward their table. Her smile was self-satisfied, and she tossed back her hair with a flick of her hand. "He left a little while ago. The bartender's a friend, but he doesn't know where he was headed. He did say Tyson has family in the area—with a ranch. Said if I wanted to find my *boyfriend*, I should head out to the Creasy ranch." She wrinkled her nose. "I had to pretend I knew who he was talking about."

"Great job, babe," Dagger said under his breath.

Seeing him lean toward her, she gave him a

dark frown. "No PDA. What if I have to come back for more information? Jeez, Dagger."

When she rolled her eyes at Dagger like he was a green hunter and should have known better, Reaper snorted. "You two girls go ahead and head to the vehicle. We'll saunter out in a bit, so we don't break your cover."

"Girls!" Carly huffed, but she rose and slung an arm around Lacey's shoulders. Then pitching her voice louder, she said, "Come on, girlfriend. No way am I letting you drive."

The two women made their way to the door, with Lacey giggling and bumping into chairs.

"She missed her calling." Reaper nodded then tossed back the rest of his beer. "Should have been an actress."

"Lacey likes smaller stages," Dagger said, a smile curving his mouth. "Let's go."

Once outside, they moved to the vehicle. The women were seated in the back, their heads close together.

Reaper was relieved. In a front seat, he'd have room for his long legs. Inside, the sound of snickering made him grin. Carly and Lacey got along like sisters, gossiping and giggling. In recent weeks, Carly had arrived home late several times after spending time with Lacey and Jamie. The women had found a love of "girl-time," where they sat with face masks "cleaning out their pores" while sharing tales of their take-downs. Carly had a sisterhood now, one she was enjoying, and he was happy for her. He wasn't exactly finding a similar "brotherhood," but he, Dagger, and Sky did get together often to watch sports, and they planned hunting and fishing trips for once the weather warmed enough. Something he really looked forward to doing. Surprising really, since he'd always been a loner.

Working with his fellow bounty hunters was a lot like being part of a tight-knit military unit. Members bonded out of necessity and a need to survive. You had to trust the people you entered into battle with. He was pretty sure the fact they were all ex-military had a lot to do with how quickly they'd meshed. Reaper had served as a Marine, Dagger was ex-Army, and Sky a Navy SEAL.

Carly and Jamie were both ex-Army...and then came Lacey—the ex-cheerleader and prom queen. Yet, she'd found a place within the group. Sure, she needed to work on her weapons' skills —they had all taken turns with her at the range, and she was getting there. And she needed to learn some hand-to-hand skills. Her idea of martial arts was her fluency with Tai Chi, but they'd come to rely on her people skills. Everyone had their place.

Jamie and Reaper, who were in charge of their satellite office of Montana Bounty Hunters, looked to add more hunters. They'd just hired Cochise—a selection all agreed was a solid one. But they needed to ramp up, because their boss at the head office in Kalispell wanted to expand. Thankfully, those were problems for another day.

At the county land management office, the women took a step back, realizing the female clerk behind the counter might be more likely to give efficient service if Dagger schmoozed the woman. She was short and round. Her brown hair was twisted into a messy knot, and her black-framed glasses were huge and thick-lensed. Her eyes were so magnified they looked enormous.

After flashing his badge, Dagger casually leaned an elbow on the counter. His gaze flickered over the woman's brass nameplate. "Miz

Moscovitz, we're hoping you can help us. We have an arsonist we've tracked to your town."

Her expression was flat. Not giving away a spark of curiosity or appreciation for Dagger's smarmy smile. A tough cookie. Reaper adjusted his sling, being sure to hide a wince.

"If you have a request, I'll need you to fill out this form." She slid a clipboard onto the counter.

Inside, Reaper chortled. Dagger was the charmer and relied on his good looks a little too much. He cleared his throat and nudged Dagger to the side. Tapping his sling, he locked gazes with the mousy woman. "Ma'am, we know you have a tough job, and probably a lot already on your plate, but the man we're looking for is dangerous."

Her gaze went to his sling then darted back to his eyes. Her cheeks turned a little pink in her pale face. "I still need the paperwork filled out."

"I understand…you have procedures. Dagger, here, will fill out your form." He shot her a tense smile. "In the meantime, I'm betting you know the people in this town pretty well. Do you know a Creasy family that owns a ranch in this area…?" From the corner of his eye, Reaper noted the way

Carly pressed her lips together to hide a smile. He aimed a glare her way then turned back to Ms. Moscovitz. "Can you help us?"

"I know the Creasys." She nodded. "They just bought a new parcel that butts up against their ranch. Do you need to see the map?"

Twenty minutes later, the group had a photocopy of the geographical contour map of the Creasys' properties.

Outside, darkness had fallen, and the temperatures dipped.

"Guess we better see about getting a room." Reaper eyed the clouds masking a full moon.

"Already handled," Lacey said, her tone cheerful. When his gaze swiveled toward her, she shrugged. "I took care of it while you sweet-talked that clerk. I reserved two rooms in a B&B."

Reaper frowned. "I didn't sweet-talk that clerk. I showed her respect."

"And she was blushing and fluttery from all that respect," Carly murmured.

Lacey giggled. "Obviously, she's into Vikings."

Reaper was glad the shadows hid the fact his face heated. "Since the rooms are settled, we should find a place to eat."

Lacey glanced at her iPhone. "I found Al's Diner. Has five stars. Good, wholesome food. That do?"

Amazing. Reaper shook his head.

Dagger laughed and patted his good shoulder. "Don't feel bad. Everyone underestimates my girl—that's part of her super-powers."

Lacey's cheeky grin gave a hint of just how smart the girl really was.

Reaper chuckled. "Carly, have I told Jamie how right she was to hire this girl?"

"Not a girl," both women chided, eyebrows drawn into frowns.

"Girl" hadn't been an accident. He grinned as he moved toward the Expedition.

AL'S DINER looked like everyone's idea of the perfect hometown café. The aromas coming out of the door before they'd even entered had his mouth watering. He and Dagger ordered big ribeyes, fried potatoes, and green beans. The women ate baked chicken, fresh green salads, and a medley of vegetables. The group was mostly silent while they ate, because all of them were hungry.

Finally, Reaper pushed back his plate. "I should call Sheriff Barron to let him know we're operating on his turf." His gaze shot to Lacey.

Shrugging, she smiled. "I'll let you handle that task, boss."

Carly gave him a sideways glance. "That's right. You and Jamie worked with the locals and the Feds chasing down that terrorist operating in the mountains here."

Reaper nodded then turned to the other couple to explain. "Jamie and her dog, Tessa, were brought in by Hank Patterson, who runs the Brotherhood Protectors. The job's how Jamie hooked up with Sky—he was working for that outfit. Afterward, they offered us both jobs, but we turned them down. We like what we do."

"Yeah, we like hunting down scumbags," Lacey said.

Before he nodded, Reaper took a breath. Those words had sounded incongruous coming from the cotton-candy confection of a woman.

Dagger's eyes danced with laughter.

"Shall we head to the B&B?" Reaper asked. "We can get started again early in the morning."

With Lacey's phone providing directions, they reached the B&B in minutes.

Ms. Kinner, who owned the place, was gracious. "Breakfast begins at seven in the morning," she said as they stood in the hallway outside their rooms.

"Ma'am," Reaper said. "I'm afraid we'll be gone sooner than that."

The older woman nodded. "Tell you what. I'll set out paper bags with bagels and muffins for you to take. I have a Keurig. Paper cups are beside it. Be sure to help yourselves."

The women gave Ms. Kinner their effusive thanks.

Reaper glanced at Dagger. "I'll send Brian the coordinates for the ranch and have him see what he can learn about the terrain and any outbuildings from satellite photos. Be ready to head out at six."

Dagger nodded and turned toward his room.

When the door closed him and Carly inside, he didn't spare a glance for the room. His gaze was on Carly, who walked nonchalantly forward and dropped their bag on the low bench at the foot of the bed.

With a glance over her shoulder, she said, "How's that shoulder?"

"Throbs." But someplace else throbbed harder.

"Oh." She sucked her bottom lip between her teeth. "Need help getting out of those clothes?"

"I'll manage," he said, keeping his tone low and even.

Her gaze slowly locked with his, and her pupils expanded. Her nostrils flared. But she turned away, keeping her face in profile. "We should probably rest. This day was really long."

She watched him. He knew it from the prickle that crawled along his skin. And she was aroused. Reaper might be bruised and aching, but in no way would he rest before he fucked her all the way to heaven.

He toed off his boots then peeled back the Velcro on his sling. He dropped it on the bench then went to work on removing his jeans and boxers. Clumsily, he unbuttoned his shirt with one hand. She still hadn't moved, but she eyed his dick, which, yeah, was rising. After all their time together, he would've thought she'd become inured to the sight, but, as always, she studied its progress.

His dick was on the big side, perfectly in proportion with his large frame—and was her favorite part of his body, although she often said she loved his eyes. Maybe because she thought she ought to like something a little less crass, but he had her number.

When he shrugged out of his shirt, he stood and walked around the bed, pulled back the coverlet and arranged pillows before he sat with his back to the headboard. Reaching for his cock, he gave himself a long, slow tug. "I'm gonna fuck you, Carly. Why aren't you already out of those clothes?"

She tossed back her head, letting her tawny-brown hair shimmer around her shoulders, and then began to remove her clothing. When her jeans, long-sleeved tee, and underwear joined the pile, she moved without an ounce of grace to the opposite side of the bed. Her movements were jerky. Her breaths rasped.

The scent of her arousal perfumed the air. Damn, she was beautiful. Full-figured. Breasts that filled his big hands. Pretty, rosy tips that were already as hard as pebbles. "Right here," he said, giving himself another stroke. "I want your pussy sliding over it."

Her breath gusted. "I love your sweet-talk."

"Don't give a shit about how sweet it is. And

you know it." He held out his right hand and gripped her hip as she straddled him. "You'll be doing all the work."

Her brows wrinkled. "But I never finish."

That was a fact. She might get them both hot, but she didn't have the stamina and much preferred him to roll her over and drive hard toward her core. "Don't think I can brace myself on both hands. Not yet. You wanna come, then you have to make it happen."

"Good thing you're so big." She centered her sex over the tip of his cock. "I can come quick." She arched an eyebrow, telling him that if she did, he was on his own.

"Huh." He reached up and slid his fingers through her silky brown hair to pull her face toward his. "Your pussy," he whispered against her lips. "*Now.*"

She acted like she didn't know where to put her hands. The left settled on his good shoulder, but the right fluttered.

"Rest it on my shoulder, babe. Closer to my neck." He winced when she did, but he gritted his teeth and didn't murmur a complaint, because his cock was so thick it felt close to bursting.

Gently gripping his shoulders, she circled her

hips, screwing herself down his length, her motions tugging and pushing on his cock, dragging it around. When she was halfway there, she gasped. "God, I love your dick."

He gave a dirty chuckle. She'd spoken loud enough, he was sure the other couple could hear her exclamation through the wall. He loved how tight and wet she was. How she squeezed all around him, sexy quivering spasms that gripped him like a tight, hot fist. "Faster," he grumbled.

"I'm in charge. And I want to savor this sensation a second. Wish you knew how it felt. So full, so hard." Her head fell back as she again swirled her hips.

He guessed he'd have to give her incentive to see things his way. Bending, he took one pretty, pebbled nipple into his mouth and sucked it like a straw. Then he teethed it, jerking back his head to tug before he let it go.

"Again," she blurted, and her thighs strained as she bobbed deeper down then up.

He rooted at her breast, teasing the tip with flicks of his tongue, before swallowing the nipple and rubbing it. When she pressed against his mouth, he opened his jaws wider and pulled inside as much of her generous breast as he could and sucked.

She bounced on his cock, which jiggled her breasts. He liked the way they felt, shivering against his skin. So, he rubbed his stubble first against one nipple then the other. Emitting moans, she moved faster, and warm liquid showered around his cock. He bent his knees and lifted his hips, moving in opposition to her downward thrusts.

The bed shook. The mattress squeaked. Their groans grew louder. He reached down with his good arm to cup her ass and drove upward, holding still at the top of the thrust, which excited her more. She ground forward and back in little jerks, rubbing her clit against the hairs on his groin. Friction built, so hot he felt it spread outward and upward, creeping across his chest and into his face. He was getting close. His balls were as hard as stone.

Reaper slipped a hand between their bodies, turning it to skim her lower belly. With a rough fingertip, he rubbed her clit, exposed because her pussy stretched around him. One hard rub, and she cried out, her head thrown back again, and her body jouncing on his cock, until her movements slowed.

When she bent to cup his cheeks and plant a soft kiss on his mouth, he felt like a conquering hero. Her gratitude was there in her soft gaze. "I love you," she whispered.

"Love you, too, babe." Then he tightened his fingers on one side of her ass and pounded upward, until he felt the explosion rip through him, and come jetted into her slick channel.

When he slowed, she wrapped her arms around his neck and snuggled her face into the corner of his neck, rocking gently against him, prolonging the sweet wave of ecstasy that lapped over them.

At last, his breaths eased to normal. He rubbed his cheek against hers. "Wish we could sleep like this. I like my dick inside you."

"I like it there, too. How about we roll?" She dragged the pillows from behind his back and lifted her body enough so he could scoot down the bed to lie flat. She followed, keeping their connection. Then, together, they slowly rolled to their sides. Resting on his right shoulder, he clamped her upper thigh between his, making sure he'd stay trapped inside her.

"Do you think they're doing this, too?" she whispered, scraping his chin with a fingernail.

He smiled. He had no doubt Dagger was busy staking his claim all over Lacey's petite frame after her performance at the bar. "Yup." Then he kissed Carly to shut her up. They both needed solid sleep before they tracked down Tyson and brought the bastard to justice.

CHAPTER 3

REAPER AWOKE. Alert. His heart thudding. For just a split second, he remembered what it was like. That this had been his life. Before Carly. He used to like rolling out of women's beds and heading home to his. He'd liked sleeping alone. Had thought only a wussy-man couldn't sleep with only his thoughts to keep him company. He stretched his body, completely occupying the space. King of his bed.

Now, he felt like something was missing. He reached out a hand, but as he'd sensed, the space beside him was empty, and the sheets were cool. The glowing digits on his watch displayed 5:00 AM. Too early to be up. Where the hell was that woman?

Turning his head, he noted a light gleaming beneath the bathroom door. Maybe she was planning on being his alarm clock. He'd enjoyed many morning wake ups feeling Carly's busy hands and mouth straying south.

Maybe he should be polite and brush his teeth. Not thinking, he rolled left, and his breath caught. Yeah, that. The arm hurt like a bitch, but the pain was a little duller than yesterday. He could manage today without the damn sling. He rose and padded to the bathroom then pressed his ear to the door. No sound emerged. He rattled the doorknob to give her time to complain if she didn't want him inside, and then entered. She was already dressed, her hair caught up in a pretty braid that trailed from the top of her head to between her shoulders, and she was applying mascara, making that strange, stretched face she made when she did the task.

He raised his eyebrows. Carly rarely wore makeup when they were on the chase. Things like sleep rated as more important.

She paused to put the wand inside the tube then pushed and pulled in rapid succession before leaning again toward the glass. "Don't look at me like that."

"Like what, babe? Man can't admire his woman?" He rubbed his chest and grinned. He thought he knew what was up, but he wanted to hear her explanation for fussing with her appearance. In his opinion, the woman was perfect as she was. Better when she was a bit mussed up and sweaty, but he didn't think she'd let him get her that way this morning.

"What?" Her gaze met his in the mirror. She wrinkled her nose. "I can't make a little effort with my appearance?"

He gripped her hips from behind and stared down at her ass, knowing she was watching him in the mirror. "You do know, the more of that you put on, the more I want to rub it off."

She rolled her eyes. "Sorry, Romeo. None of that action this morning. Lacey's always so put together, and I was feeling like a slacker."

"Lacey's…Lacey. I'll grant she's good-looking, but babe, you're no slacker." He rubbed his cock against her clothed ass. "Damn, I was really hoping you were up early, so we'd have some time for this."

She chuckled and straightened, shoving the wand in the tube and dropping it into a very fat makeup bag. Her gaze stayed on the bag. "She's always got great products, but some of them confuse the hell out of me. Highlighter for my brow bones? A contour stick to make my cheeks pop out." Frowning, she shook her head. "Did you know, she's doing all our makeup for Jamie and Sky's wedding?"

"I heard. Said since she was still broke as hell, that service would be her wedding gift."

Carly gave him a rueful glance in the mirror. "I have to confess I didn't know what the hell Jamie was thinking when she hired her."

Reaper grinned. He'd had that same thought.

"But she's good. I mean, really good, at getting information from people."

"Everyone underestimates her." He shrugged. "They don't see her as the triple-threat she really is—beauty, brains, and *pinkness*. She's pretty and sparkly, and they're all charmed—young and old."

Carly's shoulders dropped. "I can't do sparkly."

"But you can do sexy as hell." He turned her around and looped his arms behind her back. "Good thing I caught you before you painted that mouth."

She smiled while she placed her hands on his bare ass and squeezed. "And why's that?"

At her touch, he nudged his cock closer. "Because I can do this," he whispered and leaned down to kiss her. An inch from her mouth, he grimaced. "Toothpaste, first."

She laughed. "To save time, you brush, while I do this," she said, wrapping her hand around his cock and melting toward the floor.

Reaper's eyes nearly crossed when she opened her mouth and swallowed him down.

CARLY KNEW her lips were still a little swollen, but she hoped anyone looking would just think the cause was the pink gloss she'd glided on her mouth. Reaper was in a good mood. That was all that counted. She considered it her public duty to soften his hard edges before he ventured out in the world.

And yes, she'd noted he'd tossed the sling into the trash while he dressed. The spectacular blue and purple bruises on his shoulder were something else she hadn't commented on. Stubborn man.

After dressing, they'd met up with Lacey and

Dagger in the kitchen. All four filled insulated travel cups with fresh coffee and grabbed their bags of bagels and muffins Ms. Kinner had left for them on the counter, along with packets of jelly and cream cheese.

While Dagger drove, they munched and pored over the satellite pictures Brian found on Google Earth, which showed the location of the houses and outbuildings scattered throughout the Creasy property.

Reaper blew out a breath. "That's a lot of territory to cover. We might need to consider calling in some favors."

"Oh yeah, we can call Hank," Carly said. She'd heard all about Hank Patterson and the Brotherhood Protectors from Reaper.

Reaper nodded. "He's a friend with great resources. He might help us by providing snowmobiles or horses. Don't think ATVs will cut it with as much snow as is on the ground in the outlying areas."

"Better give him a call," she said. "How fast do you think he can respond?"

As it turned out, Hank Patterson, owner of Brotherhood Protectors, was as quick to react as any military commander. With the man being a former SEAL, Carly shouldn't have been surprised. Hank met the group with two large rigs hauling a horse trailer and an open-bed trailer loaded with snowmobiles.

Reaper strode toward a tall man who stood beside the horse trailer and extended his hand. "Good to see you, Hank. And thanks for this equipment. Didn't know how we were going in on foot to catch our man."

"Not a problem. We brought snowmobiles, horses, and tack." He grinned. "Guess I should have asked if you and your team know how to ride."

Reaper laughed. "Carly and I ride. Might need help with the saddle, though. Dislocated my shoulder yesterday."

Carly was surprised he'd admitted the fact, but maybe that was just another form of man-bragging.

Hank shook his head. "We'll handle getting the horses saddled. Just let us know when you need the trailer back to pick them up."

Within half an hour, two snowmobiles and two horses stood beside the road in front of a lonely gate next to the highway that opened into the Creasy ranch.

Carly wasn't worried about herself. She'd ridden since she was a kid. But she didn't think Reaper bouncing around on horseback was such a great idea. "You sure you want to ride?" she asked him.

"Only thing that's gonna take a beating is my ass, Carly. I'll be fine."

And from his gruff delivery, the discussion was over. "All right," she said, firming her lips.

"Guess we should gear up," Dagger said.

They all moved to the back of the Expedition.

For once, Carly was glad of the extra weight of her flak jacket. The air was frigid. Each breath produced a cloud of vapor. The garment provided extra insulation against the cold. They were all dressed in ski gear, insulated boots, and ski masks, which they hadn't yet rolled down to cover their faces, but they'd have to later if the wind kicked up. She had to widen her web belt and holster to fit over the extra padding. She twisted an earpiece into her ear and wore a radio strapped to her belt. Because the group was splitting up to cover more ground, they'd be out of range of the earpieces with the other half of the team.

Dagger strapped a rifle to his snowmobile and handed his Beretta to Lacey.

His frown when he did so made Carly smile. Lacey was plenty ready to bring along a weapon.

The women carried the maps, which the guys teased them about, because, "you know, women have to stop to ask for directions."

They'd already tossed a coin to determine which team would cover searching the outbuildings beside the stock pens and corrals near the ranch house. Dagger and Lacey would scour those buildings then approach the house. Reaper had spoken with Sheriff Barron the previous night and had been assured the Creasys were a law-abiding family and respectable folk. So, once they finished their search of the barns, Lacey and Dagger would approach the house and ask to search the bunkhouse and main house in case Tyson had snuck in without them knowing.

Carly and Reaper would head toward the side of the property bordered by the Crazy Mountains. The satellite picture showed a small cabin, likely used by hands when the weather turned dicey, and a rough barn which might hold hay and machinery a little farther away. They'd have the most ground to cover, and given that the terrain was more rugged, Reaper had to be relieved they'd be on horseback.

Carly stowed the remainder of their breakfast into her saddlebag and took a moment to run her hands over her horse, ending at the pretty black mare's head. "Okay, pretty girl, we're going to have ourselves an adventure today."

"Woman, you ready for this?" Reaper asked, leading his buckskin gelding up beside her.

"As ready as I'll ever be. You told me that sometimes you track skips on horseback. You made the possibility sound like a lot of fun."

He grunted. "Tell me that when this day is finished, and you've got saddle sores on your butt."

Shaking her head, she rolled her eyes. "You're such a romantic."

"And don't you know it. Who else would build his woman a koi pond in the middle of Montana?" He bent and gave her a hard kiss on the mouth. When he lifted his head, he winked. "Saddle up."

They traveled as quickly as the conditions would allow. Still, the sun was well above the tree line when they neared the cabin. They tied off their horses to low branches and hiked the rest of the way, splitting up as they neared to circle the cabin.

Reaper signaled he'd check out the outhouse first.

Carly noted no footprints around the building, but more snowfall appeared to have fallen in this area the previous night. So, she couldn't take the lack of tracks as gospel that Tyson wasn't around.

"Nothing around this side," she whispered.

"Nada here," Reaper's voice came through her earpiece. "Let's take a look inside."

She pulled her handgun from her holster and took a quick peek around the corner of the building at the front. With the area clear, she moved forward, ducking beneath the single aluminum-framed window.

Reaper approached from the opposite side, his Glock held in front of his body. He darted in front of the door and twisted the doorknob. It wasn't locked. Both took deep breaths. Reaper nodded then opened the door and stepped quickly through it, moving to the right side.

She slipped in, too, moving to the left, and scanned the area. The small living room area was empty, save for a sagging arm chair and a patio bench.

Both their gazes went to the door at the back of the narrow room, which had to lead to a bedroom.

"Ralph Tyson," Reaper called out. "Fugitive Recovery Agent. Come out with your hands up."

Not a sound.

"Flashlight," Reaper muttered.

He was right. The walls had no windows on the sides or back of the cabin. Too many shadows to see clearly into the back space. She pulled her Maglite from her belt and cupped it against her gun. Carly blew out a breath then stretched her neck, side to side, to get rid of the tension, before moving quickly through the room to the door in the back, with Reaper right behind her. She went to the left, reached out for the knob then nodded. She eased open the door.

The door moved easily—until it didn't.

Her body tensed. She moved her hands, shining the light inside, and saw a long, shiny filament of something stretched from the knob that led into the bedroom beyond. Alarm made her heart stutter. She reached out to shove Reaper to the right and leapt to the left.

A loud bang sounded, accompanied by a bright flash. Flames shot out from the door then receded quickly back. She smelled fuel—gasoline—then acrid smoke billowed outward. "Grenade," she shouted, although she could barely hear her own voice. She glanced briefly toward Reaper who staggered to his feet, then she began to run toward the front of the cabin, knowing he'd follow. By the time they reached the front door, the back of the cabin was engulfed.

Outside, they kept close to the side of the cabin, skirting around the perimeter. The outer boards in the back were hot to the touch. They raced to the tree line. Then with their backs pressed together, slowly circled, scanning outward, their weapons raised, looking to see whether Tyson had stuck around for the fireworks, but there was no sign of him.

The cabin was fully engulfed, hissing sheets of dripping ice sliding off the tin roof.

Hidden in the trees, Carly slumped against a trunk and slid downward, dragging in deep breaths. Her ears still rang. Yet, she had to call Dagger and Lacey to let them know what had just happened. She unclipped her radio and hit the talk switch. "Dagger! Dagger!" She waited a few seconds, then repeated the hail. After a moment, not able to hear whether they answered, she said, "The cabin was rigged to burn. Flash-bang grenade, I think. Probably tied to gas cans. Cabin's in flames. We both made it out. Will contact you when I can hear."

Then she sat in the snow at the base of the tree. Reaper leaned his good arm against the trunk then squatted beside her. He pressed his forehead against hers. They stared into each other's eyes. The explosion had been close. If she hadn't seen the wire…

She shook her head. No use dwelling on what hadn't happened. Her training, their combined training, helped them survive. Now, they knew they were on the right track. Tyson must be close.

CHAPTER 4

REAPER SHOOK his head and stretched his jaws to again pop his ears. His hearing was back, but a faint, irritating whooshing sound remained. By the way Carly kept rubbing her right ear, she suffered similar residual effects.

Reaper glanced beyond the tree line to where the cabin still smoldered, thick black smoke billowing into the air. He shuddered and closed his eyes, saying a quick thanks that neither of them received burns. He'd watched the flames shoot out like a flamethrower from the open doorway as he'd fallen to his back after Carly pushed him aside. They'd been lucky. No, he'd been lucky. Her quick actions had saved them both.

"I'm entering the coordinates on my GPS," Dagger said, his voice overly overloud. They'd arrived a little while ago, having already wrapped up their part of the search.

Reaper grimaced. "You don't have to shout any longer. I can hear you."

One side of Dagger's mouth quirked upward. "Good to hear—no pun intended."

"Asshole."

Both men knelt in the snow, the contour map spread on the ground before them. They'd selected a route to the barn and a spot to leave behind their horses and snowmobiles, out of hearing of anyone who might be lurking around the barn. They'd have to hike in the rest of the way.

Reaper glanced at the women.

Lacey knelt in front of Carly, using antiseptic wipes she'd produced from a pocket to gently clean away the black soot on Carly's face. Her nose wrinkled. "You look like you have a sunburn. Not bad enough to peel, I think, but I have some cream that should help with the redness."

Of course, she did. He hoped she had enough for him, too, because the skin on his face felt a little tight and hot. When Lacey moved to him, he didn't make a smartass comment. He simply closed his eyes and let her do her thing.

"I'm thankful you two won that coin toss," she said softly. "I wouldn't have recognized that tripwire for what it was."

"Now, you know," he said. "We need to review his file again. I don't remember reading about him knowing how to do anything other than strike a match." He remembered the mug shot—a scrawny-looking dude with his hair shaved close to his head. Crazy eyes.

Lacey cleared her throat. "The arson investigator was still figuring out how he did it. He knew he used an accelerant, likely gasoline, but he didn't know for sure how he set the fire."

"He wasn't looking for a flashbang grenade. He's not very good at his job." As she began slathering cream over his face, he opened his eyes and locked his gaze with hers. "We have to assume Tyson might have more tricks up his sleeve. The boy's got himself a copy of *The Anarchist Cookbook*."

"Or he's been scoping out bomb making on the internet," Dagger drawled.

"There's an actual book...?" Lacey's voice rose, her eyes rounding.

"Not legal to even own in some places," Reaper muttered.

"Huh." Lacey shook her head.

"Before your time."

"And yours," Carly said, resting a hand on his good shoulder.

Funny how he'd completely forgotten the tenderness on his left side. Now, he had bumps and bruises and a hot face that distracted from the shoulder pain. He snorted. He was looking for rainbows over the fact he hadn't been burned to death. When had he become a "cup half full" kind of guy?

He glanced up at Carly. Her cheeks were a deep pink, but otherwise, she was her same beautiful self. "You ready to do this again? We could wait for backup from law enforcement."

"John Creasy was on the horn with the sheriff when I left," Dagger said, shrugging. "He knows about the cabin. They won't be far behind."

Carly gave them both a frown. "We're not waiting and taking a chance on them getting to Tyson before we do. Uh-uh. He's our bounty."

A smile stretched his mouth, stinging his skin. God, he loved that feisty woman.

THE LAST HALF-MILE to the barn was exhausting. They kept inside the cover from the trees where the snowpack wasn't as deep. Still, Reaper could feel the muscles stretching and burning beneath the bruises. The group came to a halt, and he watched as Dagger lifted his handheld GPS device to check their coordinates.

"It's just up ahead," he said softly.

Reaper could hear him perfectly well now over the new earpiece. He'd lost his first one in the explosion, but Lacey pulled a spare from yet another pocket of her jacket. Reaper vowed to spend time with her at the gym, teaching her hand-to-hand to help complete her training. The woman was made for this job. Hell, he thought maybe she ought to be writing their standard operating procedures, because she came thoroughly prepared for almost any contingency—replacement tech, aloe vera cream for burns, pink lip gloss. That last thought made him smirk.

The team moved forward with renewed

determination, all drawing weapons, gazes trained to the white wilderness around them.

"Remember, Cupcake, stay behind me," Dagger said. "Shadow my moves."

"Sure as shit hope you're not talking to me," Reaper drawled.

Lacey chuckled. "I don't even mind anymore when he calls me that."

Reaper and Carly shared smiles. Reaper bet he knew why Dagger had chosen that name. Pretty frosting, delicious inside.

They could see the barn between the trees. Using hand signals now, Dagger indicated he and Lacey would take the barn's back door. Carly and Reaper would make their way around opposite sides to the front.

Once they began moving, dread filled his belly. The sounds of their footsteps, crunching on snow would alert Tyson to their locations. He stomped his feet, just to make sure Tyson heard him—so their quarry would come at him first. At the corner, he darted a glance toward the entrance. "Ready to move to the doors, Carly."

"I'll be right there with you."

Although he knew she was every bit as capable as he was, he wished she'd hold back.

This time, he'd get there first. Moving around the corner, he crouched low, extending his weapon, sighting upward to the closed loft then down again to the door. Carly approached, too, looking fierce with her lowered brows.

If he wasn't so scared for her safety, he knew he'd get hard. Damn, that woman.

At the door, he blocked her with his body, put his hand on the latch, and slowly opened it, checking for wire. "No wire," he said, huffing out a breath. "Ready, one…two…three." He stepped into the dim interior, heard the door at the back open, and watched a distant beam of light filter through the dust floating in the air.

With his flashlight, he scanned the nearby interior of the large structure. Hay, pitchforks, large blue barrels…

Those required further examination. He indicated to Carly to begin her search to the right. Then, with his back to the inside wall, he made his way left, around to the barrels. Relief shot through him at seeing no wires attached and nothing strapped to the exteriors. When he lightly banged on the lid of one, the barrel sounded empty. He tapped on all the rest to be sure.

Moving deeper into the interior, he shined a light upward, following with his gaze the ladder leading to the loft. "I'm checking topside."

"Hay and rope back here. A ton of tractor parts outside the door. A banged-up tractor just inside the door. Back's clear," Dagger said.

Reaper couldn't have explained why the hairs on his arms prickled upright. Deep in his gut, he had a bad, bad feeling. He stiffened. "He's not in here," he whispered. "Fuck, I think he's outside."

At the moment, a shadow darkened the front doors they'd left open. Something landed with a plop atop a large round bale. Flames burst then spread quickly, looking like liquid as it draped over the top of the dry hay. The front doors slammed closed.

"Get out the back!" he shouted.

But already he could see something just beyond the open door. Another fire licking at old machinery.

"Can't go out the back," Dagger shouted. "I'm betting he set one of his improvised bombs inside that wreckage!"

Reaper eyed the ladder. Their last route of escape, short of beating their way through the solid wooden slats at the sides of the barn.

Already, smoke filled the air. Carly coughed from her position crouched nearer the floor, and she'd pulled down her snow mask.

He pulled down his own, holstered his weapon, and climbed the ladder. At the top, he flashed around his light. "Up here. It's clear."

"We go out that loft window, he'll pick us off," Dagger said, his voice thickening.

"He's an arsonist…not a shooter," Carly gasped. "Probably doesn't have the fucking guts."

Reaper's jaw tightened. "He's desperate. He might try." He stood at the top of the ladder and held out his hand to help Lacey to her feet beside him then Carly.

Dagger came up behind her. "He's probably making good his escape."

"All the more reason we get the hell out of here."

They all converged at the large loft door that opened to the ground below.

Smoke filled the loft, choking him and burning his eyes. He slowly opened the door, his Glock aimed downward. The clearing in front of the barn looked empty. "I'll go first."

Carly clamped a hand on his arm. "You'll hand us down, or we'll all have broken ankles."

She was right. But she wasn't going first. "Dagger," he bit out.

"Right here."

"Give us cover when you get to the trees."

Gritting his teeth against the pain, Reaper knelt on one knee, grabbed the frame of the door with his left hand then reached out his right. Dagger clasped his wrist. Reaper swung his arm outward, and almost immediately, Dagger released his grip and dropped. As soon as his feet hit the ground, he began moving away from the structure.

Not much time. Heat intensified beneath Reaper's knee. He reached for Lacey, gripped her hand and swung her out, grimacing as he leaned as far downward as he could, before letting her go. "Go behind Dagger," he shouted down to her. "Keep low." She fell to her feet then her knees, pushed upward, and ran in the direction Dagger had gone.

Then he reached for Carly. They were both choking. No time for words. He gave her a nod, grabbed her hand and swung her out, then lowered her as far as he could to cut a few feet from the twelve-foot drop. When she was safe on the ground, he knew he couldn't hold the edges of the frame and lower his body. His aching shoulder wouldn't allow his arm to move above his head. He'd have to jump. Hoping his combat boots protected his ankles, he leapt.

STILL COUGHING, Carly took the direction opposite of where Dagger went. Fuck, if Tyson was out in the woods, he'd hear them coming from a mile away. Soon, she was following boot prints. Ones that pointed away from the structure. So, not theirs and moving into the trees. "I have a trail," she said.

"I'm right on your ass," Reaper growled.

Relief he'd made it out and was safe swept through her. "Not waiting."

"Don't have to. Already behind you, babe."

"On our way," Dagger said. "No tracks to the north."

She was grateful knowing Tyson hadn't laid a false trail to trick them into searching in the wrong direction. Hell, they might be lucky if he thought he'd succeeded in killing the group. He wouldn't be expecting them.

The trail led to where they'd left their horses

and snowmobiles. One of the horses was missing.

Holstering her weapon, she headed toward the big buckskin.

"No way in hell," Reaper said. "Ride with Dagger." He reached for the reins and unwrapped them from the branch where the horse had been tied. With a graceful leap, he made the saddle then leaned to the side, his gaze scanning for the trail the other horse had made. When he found it, he shot her a glance.

The look on his face made her miss a step. Reaper was all in. Tyson was his, or he'd die trying to take him down. As he whistled at his horse and gave his sides a gentle kick, his jaw firmed to granite, and he leaned close to the equine's neck, urging the horse into a gallop.

Dagger caught her upper arm in his grip. "Come on!"

She shook off a feeling of trepidation and followed him to the snowmobile. After he climbed on, she grabbed his shoulders and slid behind him. He cranked the key, and the engine roared.

"Dumbass should have disabled these," he shouted over his shoulder.

Proof Dumbass hadn't thought they'd make it out of the barn.

IN THE DISTANCE, Reaper heard the snowmobiles roar, but he wasn't slowing. He also wasn't sure the machines could follow him because of fallen branches and the fact that, so far, Tyson was sticking to the forest.

But then the trail meandered east. Into flatter terrain of cleared fields.

The path was slower going for the horse now that they moved through three feet of loose snow, but he pressed him forward, keeping as close to the tracks as he could.

After about ten minutes, he caught sight of the black mare and Tyson's gangly frame. Tyson's trail curved strangely. Maybe he'd changed his mind about heading back into the trees. His mistake brought Reaper closer.

"Ha!" He shouted at the horse, and he struck out through the fresh powder, heading in a straight line toward Tyson, who turned in his saddle.

The fugitive reined around his horse, and

then stood in his stirrups and waved. The sound of laughter echoed in the air.

Seeing red, Reaper cursed. *Crazy fucking bastard.*

And then he heard it—a horrible noise—and instantly knew why Tyson had laughed. His entire body tensed.

A groan sounded beneath the horse. His hooves were no longer muffled by dirt beneath the crunchy snow. Reaper shot a glance around him and realized the area where they stood was too flat to be earth at all. His gut tightened.

In the next moment, the ice broke. The horse began falling backward. Reaper kicked free of his stirrups, but his action was too late. He plunged into ice-cold water. The horse bumped against him. Then a hoof caught him in the side. His air expelled in a single harsh gust, and Reaper knew he was a dead man.

CARLY PEERED over Dagger's shoulder at the trail ahead when they left the trees. Finally, she could see into the distance. She tapped Dagger's shoulder and shouted, pointing past him to Reaper atop the big buckskin.

But then everything went crazy. She sighted Tyson, standing in his stirrups in the far distance. Saw Reaper's horse fall backward, sinking oddly beyond the ground. Watched water rise high into the air as horse and rider were consumed.

Dagger pulled the snowmobile to a halt at what appeared to be the rim around a flat snow-covered pond.

Carly scrambled off the snowmobile and ran as fast as the snow would allow, all the way to the edge of the pond.

Dagger caught her around the waist and pulled her hard against his chest. "Wait!" he said in her ear.

They watched in horror as Reaper disappeared. The horse fought to the surface, bouncing upward and moving toward the edge of the pond, until he got his forelegs over the edge of the ice and clambered out. Behind the hand covering her mouth, she gasped when she saw Reaper, his head bobbing above the water and his arm reaching, but not widely, for the edge of the ice.

Dagger freed her, and they both rushed to the horse. Dagger caught its reins and quickly untied a length of coiled rope from the saddle. He tied one end to the saddle horn then handed her the reins. "Stay at her head. Back her up after I get the rope around him."

Heart racing, Carly shook her head. "No. I'm lighter. I can get closer." Her gaze went to Tyson who was turning his horse, preparing to escape. "You get that bastard. Don't let him get away. Lacey and I've got this rescue."

He must have read the stubborn jut of her chin. He gave a crisp nod. "We don't have time to argue." Then his glance went to Lacey who ran up beside them.

Carly didn't have time to explain what they were doing. She left it to Dagger to quickly tell Lacey what her job was. Then he was back on his snowmobile and speeding after Tyson. She shucked her jacket and ski pants then grabbed the loose end of the rope and moved toward the edge of the ice. There, she went to her belly to better distribute her weight and low-crawled to Reaper, now ten feet away. *Not a huge distance*, she reassured herself, but she didn't like the blue pallor of his skin. When she drew nearer, she stopped because she heard ice groan. She'd be of no use to him if she fell into the water, too. "Reaper," she said. "Reaper!" she shouted louder.

His gaze met hers; his arctic eyes were dull.

"I'm throwing you the rope. You have to catch it."

"Can't...breathe. Ribs..."

She nodded. Time for tough love. "I understand, but you have to suck it up, Buttercup!" she shouted. "No pansy-ass excuses, Marine."

His lips twitched, but he gave a slow nod.

Holding the last of the coil, she reached to the side then flung the rope toward him.

Thankfully, it landed near him. On the second swipe of his hand, he caught the rope and wrapped it around his fist.

She glanced back at Lacey and moved her hand in quick jerks. "Pull his reins! Move him back!"

Too slowly, the horse moved backward. When the rope tightened, removing all slack, Reaper cried out.

Tears stung Carly's eyes as he floated closer. She scooted backward, slowly, flattened on the ice, moving inches in front of him, but holding eye contact the entire way. Then she climbed over the edge of the ice.

Reaper stayed on his belly, letting the horse drag him, the snow parting around him until he reached the bank.

There, Carly crawled to him and wrapped him in her arms. He was shivering hard, and his dampness seeped into her clothing.

"Dagger left his jacket." Lacey fell on her knees beside them.

Together, the women helped him sit then worked on getting Reaper's soaked jacket off, and then shoving his longer arms into Dagger's jacket. Carly raked off his sodden ski mask and replaced it with her own. Then they knelt on either side of him, rubbing his arms and torso to warm him up.

"We're in trouble," Lacey said, her brows wrinkled.

Carly knew it, too. Reaper wouldn't last long before slipping deeper into hypothermia.

"If we can get him on the snowmobile, you can head back to the barn." Lacey pointed over her shoulder. "It's a big fucking bonfire."

Carly nodded and shook Reaper. "You have to help us. We need to get on the snowmobile. Can you walk?"

"I'll bring it closer," Lacey said.

Reaper's eyelids fluttered open but sagged low again.

She didn't like the dazed look in his eyes. "You are not gonna sleep, bastard. You're not quitting. Marines never quit. Get the fuck up!"

"Nag...nag," he muttered.

She took heart from the fact he could tease her. "This next move is gonna hurt, Reap. We have to help you up." She signaled to Lacey, and they both stood and bent toward him.

Holding onto their arms, he dragged himself to his feet. The women scooted beneath his arms and helped him walk slowly to the snowmobile. She knew he was hurting bad when he groaned with every step.

At the vehicle, he shook his head.

"You have to lift your leg. Lean on me," Carly said, bracing herself against his almost dead weight. "I won't let you down."

"Never...do." He leaned against her then slowly lifted his leg high enough, with Lacey's tug on his boot to get it over the top.

Then Carly pushed to get his mass centered. "Now, scoot back. I'll ride in front. You have to hold me. I know you can do that, baby. You can hold me tight."

She climbed on and waited as Lacey guided his hands around her middle.

Then the other woman raced back to the edge of the pond to retrieve Carly's jacket and pants. Those, she stuffed between their bodies. "You'll need them when you get to the barn."

"What about you?" Carly said. "Want me to come back after I have him safe?"

Crossing arms over her chest, Lacey shook her head. "I'll follow their tracks. No way will Dagger let him get far. If he runs into trouble, he'll need me."

They shared charged glances. As Lacey turned and hurried in the direction Dagger had gone, Carly started the snowmobile's engine and headed back to the barn.

The journey was torturous. Every time they hit a bump, Reaper groaned loudly enough she heard him over the sound of the engine. But at last, the vehicle reached the burning barn. There, she pulled the vehicle as close as she could. Flames still licked at dry wood. The roof had collapsed. Parts of the side wall had fallen inward. The heat rolling off the burning structure was wondrous, making her realize she shivered. After a few minutes, she disengaged his hands and slid off.

Standing beside him, she cupped his face and turned it. His features were still stiff. His gaze unfocused. Worry clamped her chest. "Talk to me," she said.

He licked his lower lip, which was split. "Nearly...burned. Twice." The barest semblance of a smile curved his mouth.

"And here I am, bringing you back to an inferno." She shook her head as she moved closer. He was going to make it. She kissed his mouth then slid her cheek against his. He groaned and reached with his right hand to grip her hair. She let him turn her head then sighed when he kissed her.

When he pulled back, he leaned his forehead against hers. "Need off this thing."

With him leaning his body against hers, he dragged his leg over and stood. He swayed for a second, and she moved in closer, helping him keep his balance.

"I'd hug you, but that would probably kill you."

"Don't care," he muttered and pulled her in.

Above, she heard a familiar, thrilling sound.

They both glanced upward just as a helicopter appeared over the tops of the trees. "Guess the cavalry is here."

"No…a SEAL. Almost as good as a Marine."

She chuckled then waved to Hank Patterson as he sat with his legs over the edge of the open cabin. A ladder descended. "Think you can climb?"

"Maybe you better see if they have a basket."

Yeah, her man was in a bad way if he'd let a SEAL see him weak.

CHAPTER 5

ONCE AGAIN, Carly stood to the side in an ER treatment room, while a doctor clucked over Reaper.

The doctor glanced at the mottled, now green, bruising surrounding his shoulder then the spectacular blue bruise, in the distinct shape of a horseshoe, atop his ribs. "Man, you need a new line of work."

Reaper grunted then hissed in a quick breath.

Carly suppressed a smile. No way in hell would he give up bounty hunting. The chase and capture were in his blood. In hers, too. When every day presented new challenges, and the occasional exhilarating thrills, how could they give it up? Hunting was so much more fun than sitting tied to a desk—the reason why her writing career had stalled. Not that she held any regrets. She was living inside a romance novel and loving an actual, breathing hero, who was so much more interesting than any man she could create on the page. Still, her fingers itched for a few minutes to describe the "adventure" they'd just survived.

"How's he doing?"

She jerked in surprise at the whisper coming from so close and turned to Dagger, who'd sidled up beside her.

Lacey stood there too, holding on to his hand. She lifted her other hand and gave a flutter-finger wave. "Got here as soon as we could. We had an escort all the way to the detention center."

"Yeah." Dagger grinned. "Hank sent a couple of his guys, Kujo and Bear, to ride along."

Carly smiled. "Hank told us when we were flying here that you had Tyson. How'd that go?"

Dagger chuckled. "As soon as I got close enough, I fired a shot in the air. His horse bucked him off. When I came up beside him, he raised his hands fast."

"Can't have been that easy," Lacey drawled.

"He sported a shiner and had a busted lip when I caught up."

"Yeah, well…" Dagger gave a ferocious frown. "You don't try to kill my friends and come away without a scratch."

"Guess I missed out." Lacey waggled her eyebrows. "I do love watching you in action."

Dagger cleared his throat. "Anyway, I cuffed him, put him up on his horse, and held his reins all the way back to the gate next to the highway."

"I rode behind him." She shuddered. "On a horse. The view was a long damn way down."

"I'll give you riding lessons," Dagger murmured.

His sexy, rumbling tone said the lessons might not feature a horse. Carly grinned. "So, the horses, the snowmobile—they were all returned to Hank? He'd already left a guy at the barn to return the one we used."

Dagger nodded. "We're all done. Clear. Just have to get back to Bear Lodge to turn in the papers to Brian so we can get paid." He lifted his chin toward Reaper, who still sat hunched over on the edge of the examination table, while the doctor reviewed x-rays. "How's our guy?"

"We'll see. The doctor was pretty sure he has

a couple of cracked ribs. He should be released in a few."

"Hairline fractures. Two." The short, disheveled-looking doctor pointed toward the pictures. "No use wrapping your ribcage. You'll have to take it easy—no heavy lifting. Your body will tell you whether you're screwing up." He gave Reaper a hard stare. "Pay attention."

Reaper's mouth twisted. "How long?"

"Give yourself six weeks to get back to your normal activities."

Reaper's gaze slid to Carly. "That ain't happening."

The doctor shook his head. "I'm guessing I'll see you again, sometime. Stop at the administration desk for your release papers." With a nod toward Carly, he left.

Lacey held up a clean navy Montana Bounty Hunter tee. "Brought this. Wish we had a button-up shirt, but this one was all you had clean in your bag."

Carly took the tee and walked toward Reaper. "I'll help."

"Let's just get home," he growled.

ONE MORE TIME, Reaper was consigned to the back seat of his own vehicle. Which wasn't really so bad. Carly sat in back, too, her hand curled inside his. But she sat in the far-right seat, not the middle, and that decision bugged him.

They hadn't talked much since leaving Eagle Rock. Everyone was tired.

He glanced to the side and noted the narrow line of Carly's lips. "What?"

A brow arched as she turned and raised her head. "*What?* Can you be more specific?"

Damn, she was snippy. What the hell had he done? He cleared his throat. "You still pissed we took this job?"

She drew a deep breath. "Someone had to. They'd have had a rough go of the capture without another team, but why us? You were already injured."

He glanced outside through the passenger window. Expressing himself wasn't his strong suit. Not something he'd done much before Carly. Since leaving the Marines, he'd only ever had to answer to himself. But he guessed she deserved an answer. His eagerness to get the hell out in the field again had placed her in danger. "I didn't want to talk," he mumbled.

He heard a snicker from the front seat. No doubt Lacey was really enjoying this. Maybe more than Carly. "After I clotheslined Big Bert, I knew you'd be all over my ass."

"You are not Superman."

Wow. She must have bottled up that one, because the comment came out the second she popped the cork. "Didn't say I was."

"You didn't use your head. He was a big guy and coming in your direction with enough speed to do some real damage. You must have known the impact was gonna hurt."

He grimaced. Truth was, he hadn't really thought—he'd reacted to the situation. Done what needed doing, but if he said that, she'd only get more pissed. Ah, hell. "You're right. I didn't think." There. He'd said something contrite. Maybe now, she'd let him take a nap.

"And then about the pond…"

Oh, fuck. He remembered the anger he'd felt when Tyson had goaded him, laughing and standing in his stirrups. Already pissed because Tyson had twice tried to kill them, and his gut was churning over the fact Carly had put herself in danger to save his ass, he'd seen red—not the outline of the damn pond.

"Yeah. I should have known he had a reason for that half-circle path he took," he said, begrudgingly.

The tautness of her mouth eased. Her shoulders slumped. "I could have lost you."

The ragged huskiness of her voice squeezed his chest. He could have lost her in that cabin, too, but she'd kept her head. Ended up saving them both. He squeezed her hand. "Babe, I'm not Superman."

"No, you're not," she said, her voice trembling. She glanced away.

But not before he noticed the moisture welling in her eyes. *Oh, hell.* "Look, I know I screwed up. I can't promise I won't again. It's the way I'm made. I see a target—I shoot. But..." He sighed, rubbing his thumb over her knuckles. "I promise, I'll try to do better. I'm getting older. And right now, I hurt like hell. More important than saving myself unnecessary wear and tear, I don't want to leave you facing down a rotten fugitive on your own, because I'm out of commission."

She took a deep trembling breath and nodded. "We're taking some time off. You heard what the doctor said."

He bit back his instant protest. "I'll take a little. Jamie and I have to go over resumes."

"Which is something you can do from home. I'll pick up the files she wants you to review."

Glad she wasn't still on the verge of crying, he said, "Okay. Maybe we can catch up on stuff around the house."

She shook her head. "You are resting."

"Only way I can stay in bed is if you're there, too."

Her gaze darted toward him then narrowed on his smirk. A laugh gusted. "You're impossible."

He gave her his sexy look, narrowing his gaze on her face, and then letting it roam over her body. "I'm very possible. Whenever. Wherever."

Lacey giggled so hard she snorted.

Dagger cleared his throat. "Speaking of new hires. Cochise seems to be working out well."

Reaper hadn't worked with him yet, but Jamie said he had good instincts. "He's ex-SWAT. Six years in the Army before that. Sniper. I've been on a few cases we could've used that kind of talent."

"Have you thought about hiring someone to help out Brian in the office?" Lacey asked, glancing back. "Poor guy's there, 24/7."

Reaper was happier with the change of subject. "We've discussed it, but Jamie wants to hold off a while. She said he was a bit of recluse after he got out of rehab. He has a purpose now, and he's more social. But yeah, when things ramp up, he'll have a lot on his plate."

This time, the silence that followed was more comfortable. Reaper rested his head on the headrest and let his body relax. He was almost falling asleep when he felt Carly's fingers pull from his grasp, then she scraped her nail across his palm then up to his wrist.

Reaper liked a little scratching. Down his spine, behind his balls. He gave her a sideways glance. Was she getting eager to be home? Alone with him? Rolling his head to the side, he glanced her way.

Her gaze was locked on his face. And the pink in her cheeks wasn't all burn.

He jerked his head, telling her silently to come closer.

Carly unbuckled, and the alarm dinged. She quickly scooted over to the middle seat and buckled up again, killing the bell.

Reaper leaned toward her ear. "Open the jacket," he whispered.

Trying to do it quietly only prolonged the jagged scrape. Dagger's gaze went to the rearview mirror, meeting his. Reaper gave him a nod.

Dagger reached out and flipped up the mirror, and then turned on the radio.

Reaper angled his body so his back fit into the corner made by the door and the seat. Then he slipped his arm behind Carly and slid it around her waist. He tugged to move her body so her back rested against his chest. "Better?" he whispered against her hair.

When her hand covered his, and then guided it beneath the opening of her jacket to her breast, he smiled.

The long ride home just got more interesting. With his breaths deepening, he filled his hand with her soft breast and massaged. Before long, he felt the tip harden. Pinching it through two layers of fabric wasn't quite good enough, so he quickly slipped his hand under the shirt, flicked open the sliding fastener at the front of her bra and palmed her bare breast.

Carly's thighs crossed. Her back arched, pushing her breast harder against his hand. Taking her hint, he pinched her nipple then rolled it between his fingers, while listening to the soft hitch of her breath. Angling his arm to touch her right breast, he spent a few minutes teasing it, knowing she was getting hotter. Would she be more daring?

He glided his hand down her ribs and tapped the button on her jeans.

Her breath held. One second. Two. And then she quietly unbuttoned her jeans and slid down the zipper. This time, the rasp was masked by the music. One of Tom Petty's songs, which Lacey sang along with.

Then Carly sucked in her belly, just enough so he slid his hand into the space. She grabbed the edge of her jacket and covered his hand, to hide it should anyone look back, but her modesty didn't last long.

When he touched her clit, she jerked, her foot kicking the back of Lacey's seat.

Reaper and Carly held still for a few seconds, before he slid deeper, gathering moisture from her drenched folds and returning to her clit. Then he rubbed his fingertip in circles, while Carly pumped her hips in the softest of undulating waves. Her face turned, nuzzling into the crook of his neck. Her mouth sucked at his skin then bit.

She lifted her hips and eased the fit of her jeans, giving him just enough space to dive deeper. Now, he thrust two fingers inside her while his thumb grazed her nubbin. Without the music, he had no doubt the couple in the front would hear slippery, juicy sounds, because his fingers pumped into a well of heat.

Reaper wanted to groan. His cock was so hard it stretched the left leg of his jeans, the fabric irritating him beyond belief. More than anything he wished he could pop open his pants and set it free in the warm cozy air inside the SUV. He wished he could drag Carly over his lap and fuck her. Maybe Dagger and Lacey wouldn't have minded, but he'd never embarrass Carly in that way.

In front, a ding sounded. A turn signal. Carly didn't notice, but Reaper glanced between the seats and saw Dagger was turning into a roadside motel. Reaper's laughter stirred Carly, who murmured like a kitten then drew back her head.

"What?" she mumbled.

"Zip up, babe." He withdrew his hand.

Minutes later, with a key in his hand and Carly's hand tucked into the back of his waistband, Reaper opened the door to their room. Dagger hadn't bothered looking up from the paperwork he'd been filling out before he'd tossed the key at Reaper and barked, "Two hours!"

That might be enough time. He was still grinning after the clerk asked them whether they were sure they wanted two rooms. Carly's face had blushed beet red, while Lacey's eyebrows rose nearly to her hairline.

Inside the room, Carly kicked off her boots, shoved down her jeans and underwear, and left them on the floor. With flick of her hand, she cleared the bed of the covers and sprawled on the mattress.

Reaper didn't bother with his boots. He opened his belt, pushed his jeans past his hips and eased down over her and rested on his right hand, while nudging her center once before pushing inside. At the moment, he didn't give a fuck about his shoulder or his ribs. He was inside her, sliding deep, surrounded by slick heat.

"How'd they know?" Carly asked, her voice breathy.

"Don't give a fuck. Put your legs around me." He rested his weight on his elbows, tucked close to his body to prevent any unnecessary jarring. Then he stared down at her face and began to move.

Carly was careful, too, keeping her hands pressed against his chest, but moving her hips to meet his thrusts.

"Goddamn!" He groaned and gave her a frown. "I'm not gonna last. So fucking tight."

She grinned and squeezed her muscles around him. "You're just so fucking big."

"Spoiled you, haven't I?" One corner of his mouth kicked up.

"For any other man? Hell, yeah." When he thrust again, she closed her eyes. "Feels *sooo* good."

Gritting his teeth, he stroked faster, enjoying the building heat. When her moans came closer and closer together, he paused.

Her eyelids lazily blinked open.

Reaper locked his gaze with hers, making sure she knew he was dead serious about what he would say. "Babe, the next time you see a trip wire," he said, pitching his voice low and deadly, "*do not* take time to shove me out of the way."

She swallowed, and her eyes filled. "I…c-can't promise that."

"Carly," he growled.

"I *won't* promise."

"*Carly…*" He clenched his jaw.

Reaching up, she laid her palms against his cheeks. "Would you make me the same promise?"

His body shivered with tension. He couldn't answer that. Of course, he wouldn't.

"I don't love you any less than you love me."

He breathed out and lowered his head. "Damn you," he whispered.

Carly's next breath was ragged. She lifted his face, kissed his cheek then his mouth. "We're the same person, Reaper. Maybe I don't have the muscle, but deep down, we're the same. I'd die for you. Don't want to, but I won't hesitate if *not* acting means I'll endanger you."

"Maybe I should give some thought to what the doctor said," he muttered.

"About finding another line of work?" She snorted. "You go ahead and quit. I don't plan to. Then who'll have my six?"

His gaze narrowed. "I'm gonna have to keep one step ahead."

Tilting her head to the side, she pursed her

lips. "Maybe." She gave him another sexy squeeze. "Or maybe you'll have to keep me so worn out, I'll always be dragging my ass behind yours."

He grunted. "Think that might work?"

"Let's see." She smiled.

Reaper began moving again, with even strokes. Over and over. Never varying the angle or the speed. With the slow pace, he could withstand the dull ache.

At first, Carly's expression was defiant, and her lips pinched firm. She didn't move or do anything except hold his gaze. But gradually, her breaths shortened, and she was forced to open her mouth. Then she initiated moves, arching her back and spreading her hands to fist in the sheets, rolling her hips to meet his thrusts. "Faster, damn you!" she bit out.

Reaper smiled, but only marginally increased his pace. Who thought he was Superman now?

"Bastard."

As he sucked in a breath, he shook his head.

"Fucker," she whispered harshly.

He jogged his eyebrows. "Guess so. I am fucking you."

She let go of the sheets and smoothed her hands over her belly and lower.

Not getting away with that. Reaper thrust inside and held.

Carly rolled her eyes and slid away her hands.

He pulled free, not wanting to admit he had to because breathing was becoming impossible. Easing to the mattress, he lay on his back. "Come here."

Carly moved toward him and shoved down his pants a little farther before swinging a leg over his hips. "*I* won't tease," she said, chiding him.

"I won't complain."

She gripped his cock and slowly lowered her body, consuming him. Then she raised and lowered, raised…faster and faster. As she moved, she stripped away her shirt and bra, and then bent over him, tempting him with her jiggling breasts. He couldn't resist, cupping them and squeezing as she moved forward and back, her movements shorter and harder.

"Close," she gasped.

As his heart pounded, he twisted her nipples. "Finish it," he rasped.

She powered down, jerking forward and back, her cries breaking from her throat.

Enthralled with his wife, Reaper just watched. She was so ferocious, so passionate. His balls were cramping, ready to explode, but he wanted her there with him. Dropping one hand, he touched her clit, and the reaction was like he'd hit a switch.

She cried out, pumped twice, then swayed, her eyes squeezing shut as her pussy rhythmically clasped him.

Reaper gave a shout and gripped her hips, forcing her to grind against him. His release was so powerful that pain exploded in his side, but he held his breath, his shoulders rolling off the mattress to curl toward her, as he wrung the last bit of pleasure. Then he collapsed backward.

When she opened her eyes, she began to fall toward him.

Instead, he raised his right hand to stop her. "Beside me."

Understanding had her blinking her eyes, and she pulled free and cuddled against his uninjured side. They rested together, not sleeping.

After a while, she turned her head. "Are we okay?" she asked in a small voice.

"Am I happy about what you did? No. And I know you're still pissed about me taking this job." He met her glance. "I think, we'll probably get pissed with each other again, but I think we're just fine."

She sighed and trailed her nails over his belly, absently, like she didn't know she was. "I love this job, Reaper, but if you want me to quit, I will."

He grabbed her hand and threaded his fingers with hers. "I don't want you to. You're a great partner. A solid hunter." He swallowed past the lump in his throat. "Besides, I'd probably get partnered with that new guy, Cochise. Can you imagine?"

A wide smile stretched across her mouth. "Every female you questioned would be happy as hell to talk to you both. You'd be perfect bookends—you're both so tall, one dark, one blond. The pair of you would probably get invitations for threesomes on a daily basis."

He wrinkled his nose. "*That's* where your mind goes?"

"It does, when I have this pointing my way." She gripped his already recovering cock in her fist.

He glanced down at her fist, which was beginning a sexy push-pull motion. "How will we fill the time while those two get it on?"

She snorted and started giggling. "Wish I could hear what they're saying about what we did."

Reaper blew out a breath as he stared down at her hand. His cock felt near to bursting. "You don't think Lacey'll spill at your next girls' night?"

"Now, why would you think we'll talk about sex?" Her eyebrows arched high.

"Because Lacey tells Dagger every damn thing you ladies say, and Dagger can't wait to embarrass the hell out of me and Sky."

"Well, I better have a really great story to share," she said, moving to her knees and bending over him.

Reaper threaded his fingers through her soft hair and stared at the ceiling. Not counting the bumps and breaks, his life was pretty damn good. Despite the fact she'd scared the hell out of him today, Carly was the only partner he ever wanted.

CHAPTER 6

SITTING in the open bullpen of the Montana Bounty Hunters' office, Reaper felt edgy. After a week of easy captures—mostly folks who'd failed to show up for court-ordered drug testing and tried hiding in their friends' apartments—he was ready for a real job. His shoulder no longer sported any bruises. The pain in his side had stopped causing him to suck in his breath at every jarring move. Carly still watched him with an eagle eye for any sign of weakness. At the end of their work days, she'd run him a hot bath with Epsom salts and hand him a cold beer for a long soak. He might actually miss the coddling when she decided he was healed enough to take care of himself.

Now, he stared at the folder Brian handed him for one Martina Claxton, a woman who'd flipped the bird at the system, because she didn't want to pay a stack of traffic tickets. She'd missed her court date with the judge. He glared across at Brian whose expression looked entirely too cheerful. "Seriously, dude?"

"Jamie says Carly gets to say when you're ready for the tougher assignments." He angled his head toward Carly who stood near the counter with the Keurig along with Lacey, their heads bent close together.

He figured they were likely talking about "the wedding."

"Hey, Carly," Reaper said, raising his voice. When she glanced his way, he lifted the folder and shook it. "Babe, Martina Claxton, seriously?"

Carly leaned toward Lacey and said something. The two laughed. Then Carly sauntered toward him, a smile gracing her face. "Seven hundred dollars for one day's worth of work. The job'll be easy."

The money wasn't the issue. The lack of action was. He needed something that got his blood stirring, because he was bored as shit. "I don't want easy." Damn, his voice was a whine.

And now Brian grinned like a mad clown. *Fuck*. "You know I'm ready, babe. How about we leave this one to the new guy?"

"Cochise is working with Sky and Jamie today," Brian said. "Some guy wanted for manslaughter. Skipped court and told his friends he was heading to Canada."

He tightened his grip on the folder. "So, why aren't we on that one?"

She stepped her fingers across his shoulder before digging a nail into his left shoulder.

He didn't flinch. "Told you, I'm fine," he bit out.

Leaning over, she tapped his ribs.

He blinked. Dammit, he hated being reminded of his weakness. "It's nothing."

"Not what you said when you wanted me on top last night."

"La-la-la," Brian sang and quickly rolled away.

"I didn't want you on top last night because my ribs hurt, I wanted to watch your tits. You know I like how they bounce and jiggle."

"Heard that." Dagger strolled through the front door with a sack of goodies from Gladys Morton's bakery.

"You bring kolaches?" Carly asked, her eyebrow raised.

"Of course." He nodded with a smirk. "And jeez, can you two manage to avoid talking about sex for five minutes?" he said in an overloud whisper.

Reaper narrowed his eyes but decided not to rise to the bait. He returned his attention to Carly who was already reaching into the bag. She withdrew one, bit into it, and sighed. "God, Reaper, you really should try one."

"When I want a wiener in a pastry, I'll ask you to bake it, babe."

"Gah," Dagger said, his face screwed up in disgust. "The awful pictures in my mind. I can't unsee that." He walked toward a chortling Lacey.

Carly took another bite and closed her eyes in exaggerated ecstasy. "Mmm-mm. These are Polish wieners. Not sure how a Norwegian sausage would taste in my bread dough."

This time, he screwed up his face in disgust. Her innuendo didn't sound the least bit sexy. With the rest of the office laughing their asses off, he shoved up from his seat, the file fisted in his hand. "Be in the Expedition in five."

Throughout the drive to Martina Claxton's

house, he maintained his silence, feeling as though his manhood had somehow been dented and dinged. "Next case better be something challenging. No more shit like this."

"All right."

Her agreement came way too fast. He darted a glance her way, noting her blank expression. "What? No argument? Not insisting I have to wait the full six weeks?"

She shrugged and shot him a wide-eyed look. "I figure a week of the 'shit jobs' has taught you a lesson. You won't want to clothesline some dude or race across a frozen pond on a horse, because now you know the consequences."

He grunted. Yeah, so he'd been thinking the same thing all week. But he wasn't about to give her the satisfaction of hearing him say it out loud.

"That's her place," Carly said, pointing with her second kolach toward the nice two-story brick house.

Letting the engine idle, he noticed a Lexus parked in the driveway. "Looks like she can afford to pay a ticket or two. Wonder what's up with the woman."

"Brian made the calls. Shared that she's pissed

at the sheriff. Ran his opponent's campaign, and now she claims they're out to get her. She's threatening a lawsuit for harassment."

"Was she speeding?"

"Uh huh. Tons of witnesses on hand when she cussed out the deputies every time she was pulled over," she said putting the last bite of the pastry in her mouth. "And she's been driving on an expired license. Said renewing it was a violation of her civil rights."

He shook his head. He'd never understand women. "How'd she figure that?"

"She's one of those people who thinks the government's too far up in their shit."

He frowned. "Will she pull a gun on us when we show up on her doorstep?"

She stared out the window toward the house. "The sheriff warned that she might put up some resistance."

Reaper perked up, giving the house a closer look. "Maybe this job'll be more interesting than I thought." From the corner of his eye, he watched as her grin stretched.

"Thought you might think so."

He waggled his eyebrows. "Shall we give her the full treatment?"

"Sheriff said he'd ignore her if she tried to press charges for busting down her door."

"God, I love small towns," he murmured, unable to suppress a smile.

"Small Montana towns, anyway."

Reaper parked in front of a house two away from Martina's. At the back of the vehicle, they dressed in their full gear, strapping on Kevlar vests and web belts. He carried the shotgun filled with bean bag rounds. Not that he intended it for anything other than intimidation, but the orange stock should give the woman pause.

When they were ready, Carly held out the plastic case with the ear pieces.

"Give me your lock pick kit," he said.

"You mean you're not kicking down the door?" she asked, arching a brow.

"Not if I can spare an ankle," he said dryly. *See, woman? I'm a changed man.*

Carly plucked her kit from her web belt, handed it over, then grabbed the back of his hair, her hand fisting in his ponytail to bring down his head for quick kiss. "I'll take the back door."

So, maybe he wasn't going after a high-dollar arsonist with a crappy sense of humor. He could make this work, according to his new philosophy

—no unnecessary roughness. He gave her a wink. "Let's go."

Dressed in jeans, thick black overcoats over their Kevlar, combat boots, and web gear, they headed out to snag the anti-government, or at least anti-sheriff, Martina. They walked at a fast clip, until Carly peeled away to move between the houses. At the privacy fence gate in the back, she gave him a little salute and disappeared inside.

"I'm at the back door," she said a minute later. "Door's unlocked back here. This takedown is your show."

He climbed the porch, watching the nearby windows. No curtains moved. He hoped he had the element of surprise. Given the sheriff thought she might resist, he didn't want her barricading herself inside some room—or pulling a gun. Better to take her by surprise—and they did have the right to enter as they wished. She'd lost the right to keep them out when she'd failed to show up for court.

Kneeling in front of the door, he made quick work of the lock and stood. He began the countdown in a whisper. On "three," he twisted the lock and entered the foyer. Dragging in a deep breath, he prepared to shout.

A large figure rushed him from the left, letting out an ear-shattering scream.

Before he could adjust his stance, he was hit with a huge weight. Pain exploded in his side, and he went down and the shotgun went flying, but not before he wrapped his arms around his assailant and took her along with him. He knew the person was a she because she wore enough perfume to gag a cat.

On the hardwood floor, she fought to wriggle from his hold.

But Reaper held tight, not letting her go.

Footsteps pounded from the back of the house. "Fugitive Recovery Agent!" Carly shouted, and then she grabbed for the woman's waist and pulled to get her away. With Martina's legs kicking, knocking his shins and Carly's knees, Carly toppled onto the two already on the floor.

As he tried to suck in enough air, Reaper saw stars. Despite his wheezing, he squeezed his arms harder, hoping to still her movements, but she wriggled like a frenzied eel. Her knee caught him in the balls, shooting pain through his body. He sucked in an even sharper breath. "Fuck!" he bellowed.

"Tell me how that's working for you, hon," came a calm voice from close by.

Reaper darted a glance at a skinny man wearing a robe and house slippers and holding a newspaper and a cup of coffee in his hands. "You, Mr. Claxton?" Reaper bit out.

"Not sure I want to admit to that fact right this second."

"Can you tell her to stop moving?" He gritted the words through clenched teeth.

He sighed. "Martina? I think these people aren't letting you go. Told you, you should have apologized to the deputies."

"Not…paying…those…fucking…tickets," the woman said in a growling tone.

"Talk to the freaking judge," Carly muttered, getting her arm around the woman's neck. "Don't wanna choke you, bitch."

Suddenly, Martina's struggles slowed. Her breaths were labored like she'd run a race. She extended her arms upright in surrender.

"Could you do that after you get off me?" Reaper said, his voice embarrassingly weak.

"What's your problem?" Martina lifted her head to stare into his face.

"Ribs. Broke 'em."

"Ha!" she said, grinning.

"Oh lord," said her husband, "you're gonna get an assault charge, too."

Reaper knew she wasn't. Any good lawyer would say she was defending herself from intruders since he hadn't had time to announce himself before she hit him.

Carly sat on Martina's thighs and reached for the other woman's hands, one at a time, cuffing her. Then she roughly rolled her off Reaper. Afterward, she bent at the waist, sucking in deep breaths before reaching out to help him up.

With his dignity already in tatters, he waved away her hand and rolled in the opposite direction, groaning as he came to his feet. He plucked his weapon off the floor. Damn lot of good it had done.

Carly cleared her throat. "Do you need to go back to the ER?"

He rotated his shoulder, the movements pulling at his ribs, and he winced. Now that the woman's weight wasn't on him, he was sore, but not the stabbing pain that took away his breath. "I'm okay." Then he scowled at Martina. The woman had to have thirty pounds on him. He could have kicked himself for not paying attention to her physical description when he'd scanned the file.

He glanced up at Mr. Claxton, whose lips pressed together, while laugh lines crinkled around his eyes. "We're taking her to the jail."

Mr. Claxton shrugged. "I suppose she'll stay there until the judge gets her case on his docket." His gaze went to his wife. "You be sure to tell Charlie hello." With that, he turned and headed back toward the back of the house, likely to finish his coffee in peace.

Between himself and Carly grabbing an arm, they helped Martina to her feet.

"Car's not far," Carly said, eyeing the woman's slippers. "Your toes'll get warm again once we're on the way."

Martina's mouth pursed in a mutinous frown. "I'm suing you."

Feeling better now they had their bail-jumper in custody, he shrugged. "You can try."

Later, Reaper stood in the living room of his

home with Carly. He could hear her still talking on the phone with Brian while she moved around the kitchen, preparing their lunch. She had the phone on speaker mode, so he heard Brian's loud laughter as she described their takedown of Mrs. Claxton.

While he had time, he quickly started a fire in the fireplace and stripped. By the time she ended the call and entered the room, he was nude and sitting on the leather sofa.

"I'm guessing we're not turning in our paperwork until well after lunch?" she asked, one fine brow arching. Her gaze went to his left side. "No new bruises. Aren't you glad you were wearing your Kevlar?" She set down a tray filled with roast beef sandwiches, sliced carrots, and tall beakers of water on the coffee table.

"Didn't want crumbs on my clothes," he said, grinning.

"Good thinking." She quickly stripped and joined him.

They ate their fill, and then he leaned back and patted his thighs.

Smiling, she slid across the cushion and turned to straddle his legs. When she'd worked her way down so that their groins were flush, she wrapped her arms around his neck. "That capture was fun."

He chuckled. "The glamorous life of a bounty hunter."

"Sometimes, not so much," she quipped, but then she began to move. While she raised and lowered, she bent to trail her mouth across his cheek. "Brian has something new. Needs a big team."

Watching her tits made every muscle in his body tense, but his interest was equally piqued by what she'd said. He gripped her hips to hurry her along. "Tell me more."

She gasped when he thrust her hips downward. "A drug dealer…making a run for it. Left Whitefish and is heading our way."

"Better hurry, then," he smiled, noting how hard she fought to keep her attention on the conversation now. Her eyelids were fluttering.

"Dagger and Sky…are already packing the van…while Brian makes a few last calls. They'll be here in…" She glanced at her watch then moaned. "Fifteen."

Reaper stood and walked with her toward the wall. There, he waited as she secured her ankles behind his back before he began fucking her in earnest. Heat built quickly as she rubbed her sweet breasts against his chest and sank a hand between their bodies to toggle her clit.

"You lock the front door?" he asked, giving her bottom lip a bite.

Her eyes widened, and she shook her head.

Reaper laughed. "We better make a lot of noise, or we'll have company."

"Think that will stop them?" she said, then gasped again as he changed the angle of his upward thrusts.

"Not a chance." Not that he really cared. He wouldn't stop until they both came hard.

ALSO BY DELILAH DEVLIN

For more stories featuring Montana Bounty Hunters, read:

Big Sky SEAL

Head over SEAL

Reaper

Dagger

Cochise

ABOUT DELILAH DEVLIN

Delilah Devlin is a *New York Times* and *USA TODAY* bestselling author with a rapidly expanding reputation for writing deliciously edgy stories with complex characters. She has published nearly two hundred stories in multiple genres and lengths, and she is published by Atria/Strebor, Avon, Berkley, Black Lace, Cleis Press, Ellora's Cave, Entangled, Grand Central, Harlequin Spice, HarperCollins: Mischief, Kensington, Kindle, Kindle Worlds, Montlake Romance, Running Press, and Samhain Publishing.

You can find Delilah all over the web:
WEBSITE
BLOG
TWITTER
FACEBOOK FAN PAGE
PINTEREST

Subscribe to her** newsletter **so you don't miss a thing!

Or email her at: delilah@delilahdevlin.com

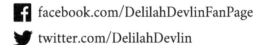

facebook.com/DelilahDevlinFanPage

twitter.com/DelilahDevlin

ORIGINAL BROTHERHOOD
PROTECTORS SERIES

BY ELLE JAMES

Brotherhood Protectors Series

Montana SEAL (#1)

Bride Protector SEAL (#2)

Montana D-Force (#3)

Cowboy D-Force (#4)

Montana Ranger (#5)

Montana Dog Soldier (#6)

Montana SEAL Daddy (#7)

Montana Ranger's Wedding Vow (#8)

Montana SEAL Undercover Daddy (#9)

Cape Code SEAL Rescue (#10)

Montana SEAL Friendly Fire (#11)

Montana SEAL's Bride (#12) TBD

Montana Rescue

Hot SEAL, Salty Dog

ABOUT ELLE JAMES

ELLE JAMES also writing as MYLA JACKSON is a *New York Times* and *USA Today* Bestselling author of books including cowboys, intrigues and paranormal adventures that keep her readers on the edges of their seats. With over eighty works in a variety of sub-genres and lengths she has published with Harlequin, Samhain, Ellora's Cave, Kensington, Cleis Press, and Avon. When she's not at her computer, she's traveling, snow skiing, boating, or riding her ATV, dreaming up new stories. Learn more about Elle James at www.ellejames.com

Website | Facebook | Twitter | GoodReads | Newsletter | BookBub | Amazon

Follow Elle!
www.ellejames.com
ellejames@ellejames.com

facebook.com/ellejamesauthor
twitter.com/ElleJamesAuthor

Made in United States
Troutdale, OR
01/04/2024

16697002R00070